AFRICAN FOLKTALES FOR THE YOUNG AT HEART

AFRICAN FOLKTALES FOR THE YOUNG AT HEART:

Hausa Tales of Wit Wisdom and Wonder

Abubakar Yusuf Ibrahim

Illustrations by Malachy Nwabuzor

ISKONCHI
African Perspectives

Published in 2025 by Iskanchi Press
info@iskanchi.com
https://iskanchi.com/

Hardcover: ISBN 978-1-957810-25-6
Paperback: ISBN 978-1-957810-26-3

Printed in the United States of America

About Iskanchi Press

Iskanchi Press is a US-based publishing house for African writing. We believe stories and ideas convey humanity to the future and that our progress to a better world is sooner achieved when all perspectives are heard and considered.

Our mission is to promote authentic African perspectives through a variety of books, including fiction, non-fiction, and children's literature written in, or translated into, English. We aim to redress the negative presumptions about Africa, satisfy the reader's interest in diverse expressions, and serve the needs of African immigrants and People of Color interested in seeing a more nuanced representation of their experiences.

Whether you're an avid reader, a bookstore owner, or a library representative, your engagement helps fulfill our mission. Thank you for being a part of our community and helping us promote diversity and inclusivity in literature.

To learn more about Iskanchi Press, discover upcoming releases, and stay updated on author events, please visit our website at www.iskanchipress.com and follow us on social media:

Browse our catalog
on Edelweiss

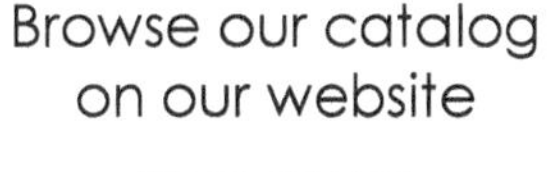

Contents

1.

The Mosquito, The Hand And The Ear

A long, long time ago, in the time of our ancestors, when animals and body parts could talk and live together like people, there lived three good friends: Mosquito, Hand, and Ear. The three friends lived together in a large compound, but each had their own little house.

The three friends worked in the village. The Mosquito worked at the meat shop, the Ear worked as a spy for Sarki, the village head, and the Hand worked in the funeral home. All three went to their different jobs every day and returned in the evenings.

They went to work as usual one day, but Hand returned early. He had not eaten anything all day and was very hungry. When he got home, he looked everywhere in his kitchen but found no food. Worse still, he had no money, not even to buy a small bowl of *tuwo* or even one *masara*.

"Kai," Hand exclaimed as his stomach growled and rumbled. When he could no longer bear the hunger, he decided to go and get some from his neighbors. "Ear always has plenty of food," he said to himself. "I will go ask him for some."

When Hand reached Ear's door, he remembered that Ear had not returned from work. None of his two neighbors were back yet. Hand sighed as his stomach growled even louder. He could not bear the hunger anymore.

He looked around the compound carefully, making sure that nobody was there. Quietly, like a cat stalking a mouse, Hand pushed the window open and climbed into Ear's House.

In the kitchen, he found a pot of food and quickly began to eat. He ate and ate and ate until he was full. Just as he was about to leave the house, he remembered that he had no food back home. He decided to carry the entire pot of Ear's food to his own house to eat later when he got hungry again.

As soon as Hand came out of Ear's apartment with the stolen pot of food, he saw the Mosquito, who had just entered the compound. Hand froze with the pot of soup still in his hands as they stared at each other.

"Ya! Hand, what are you doing? Ear is not home...Are you... Are you stealing?" Mosquito asked in surprise.

Hand began to stammer. "I was hungry...I didn't have any food. Hunger was beating me like a *ganga*. Please don't tell Ear."

Mosquito crossed his arms. "But stealing from our friend? That is not right, Hand!"

“I know. I know. Please don’t tell him. It won’t happen again, I swear.”

After some back and forth, Mosquito agreed and promised not to tell Ear.

Many moons passed, and all was well in the compound. But then one day, Hand and Mosquito quarreled over something they couldn’t resolve.

“Okay then,” Mosquito threatened in anger, “I am going straight to Ear to tell him who stole his food that other day!”

But as Mosquito flew to reach the Ear, Hand reached out like lightning and slapped Mosquito away. Again and again, each time Mosquito tried to get to Ear, Hand would swat him away.

And so, it continues to this very day.

2.

You Will Reap What You Sow!

In a village not far from here lived a man named Goni. Goni had lost his job and could no longer work because of his poor health. He eventually lost his home and became a homeless beggar on the streets. Goni wandered from door to door and from shop to shop, asking kind-hearted people for a little food or a few coins.

Goni became well known in the village, especially for his weird way of expressing gratitude to those who gave him alms or food. When other beggars received alms from people, they would say, "May God bless you" or "May your wealth increase." But whenever someone gave Goni food or alms, Goni would look them in the eyes and say, "You will reap what you sow." Then he would turn and continue on his way. Most people found Goni's strange saying amusing and were never bothered by his unusual words of gratitude, except for Lady Bebi.

Lady Bebi owned a busy restaurant in the center of the village. Her food was delicious, her business was successful, but her heart was not always kind. Each time Goni came to her restaurant and received leftovers, he would say thank you in his usual way: "You will reap what you sow." But unlike others who heard wisdom or humor in Goni's saying, Lady Bebi heard only threats and accusations. Because of this, Lady Bebi did not want to see Goni the beggar anywhere near her restaurant.

“That beggar likes to mock me,” Lady Bebi would say to herself. “I will teach him a lesson very soon.”

One day, Goni came to Lady Bebi’s restaurant to beg for food as usual. The place was busy with hungry customers, but Lady Bebi noticed him at once.

“I will teach this beggar a lesson today,” Lady Bebi muttered.

“Wait there,” she called to him with a smile that did not reach her eyes. “I have something special for you today.”

Lady Bebi went into the kitchen, to an inner room where no one could see her. She prepared a dish of food and mixed in some terrible poisons. After a moment, she came out and handed Goni the dish.

Goni bowed and received the dish with both hands. “You will reap what you sow,” he said as he received the food from Lady Bebi.

Goni went to sit under the shade of the baobab tree to eat the food. As he was about to start eating, a group of young boys came running toward him, laughing and playing.

“Ah, young ones!” called Goni. “Are you hungry? Would you like to share this meal with me?”

“Yes, yes!” the children cried eagerly, for they had been playing since morning.

Goni handed them the dish, watching with a gentle smile as they ate all the food. When they finished, Goni said, “Please return this dish to Lady Bebi at the restaurant. It belongs to her."

The boys thanked Goni and ran off towards the restaurant.

At the restaurant, Lady Bebi was pleased with herself. She was telling her friend about the little mixture she had added to Gobi's food. "That will teach him a lesson," Lady Bebi said. "Now I won't have to hear his annoying words anymore."

Lady Bebi was still bragging about what she had done when the boys rushed into the restaurant with the dish.

"Mama, we brought back your dish," one of them said, breathlessly.

Lady Bebi immediately recognized the dish, and her smile vanished.

"Where did you get this? What happened to the food?" she demanded.

Before the boys could answer, the younger son clutched his stomach and began to vomit violently. The older child also started vomiting and crying out in pain.

"Help! Help my children!" screamed Lady Bebi, realizing that her sons had eaten the poisoned food she gave to Goni. As the terrible truth dawned on her, Lady Bebi's wails echoed through the village. She tore at her clothes and threw dust upon her head in grief, crying out again and again:

"I have reaped what I have sown! I have reaped what I have sown!"

3.

How Billy Goat Scared Off The Hyena

Deep in the farthest parts of Hausaland, the Hyena built herself a nice house to keep herself cool from the heat of the Savanna. She was so very proud of the house and rarely left it except to hunt for food. She liked that the house was so far off the common path that no one stopped by to bother her. She had just one neighbor, the Monkey, who lived further down, past the anthill near the baobab tree.

The Hyena was friendly with the Monkey because they were neighbors, and it is always good to be friendly with one's neighbors. When the Hyena went off to look for food, she would often ask the monkey to keep an eye on the house until she returned. "Neighbor!" she would say to the Monkey, "I must go in search of food. Please keep watch over my house until I return."

On the far side of the Savanna lived Billy Goat, his wife, and their three children. They were a simple and happy family who kept to themselves and loved to chew on the grass and shrubs that grew in the Savanna.

One day, Billy Goat took his family on a journey to visit relatives in a distant village. Their visit was pleasant, filled with good food and warm company. As evening approached, Billy Goat and his family bid farewell to their relatives and started their journey home.

"We'll be back before nightfall," Billy Goat assured his wife.

But as they trekked across the Savanna, Billy Goat's wife got more worried as night drew nearer and their home seemed even farther.

"Billy Goat," said his wife with concern, "I think we've missed the way. These trees don't look familiar."

"I know exactly where we are," Billy Goat said confidently. "We will be home soon."

As they wandered for another hour without sign of their home or familiar landmarks, his wife finally stopped walking.

"Billy Goat, admit it. We are lost."

Billy Goat's shoulders slumped slightly. "Indeed, we are," he reluctantly agreed. "We are lost. But I will find us shelter for the night, and tomorrow we will find our way home."

Just as night fell, they spotted a house standing alone and inviting. It was Hyena's beautiful little house.

"Look there!" exclaimed Billy Goat. "Perhaps someone kind lives there who might shelter us for the night."

Billy Goat walked over and knocked on the door. He knocked and knocked but no one answered because Hyena had gone out to hunt for food. Billy Goat pushed the door and it opened.

Monkey, however, heard the knock. He hurried down from where he had been keeping an eye on Hyena' s house.

"Who are you?" the Monkey asked. "This is Hyena's house, and she is away now. You must leave at once."

Billy Goat thought quickly. It was getting dark, and his family was tired. Perhaps, they could stay here for the night since the Hyena was away. Billy Goat made a bold decision.

"Hyena's House? You must be making a mistake," Billy Goat said. "This is my ancestral home, built by my grandfather, Warlord the Goat, hero of the Savanna Wars. I have returned to claim what is rightfully mine."

The Monkey scratched his head, confused. Hyena had asked him to keep an eye on her house, but he didn't want to get into any trouble. He decided to go mind his own business and wait until Hyena returns.

"Billy Goat, what are you doing?" his wife asked anxiously

as the Monkey left. "If this is the home of the Hyena, then we must leave at once.

"Trust me," Billy Goat whispered back. "I have a plan that will save us all. Here is what we must do..."

In a short while, the Monkey saw Hyena coming and decided to warn her.

"Erm... you have some goats in your house," the Monkey said. "Just wanted to let you know."

"Goats? In my house?"

"Yes. One of them said he is Billy Goat, Grandson of Warlord the Goat."

"Billy Goat? Grandson of Warlord the Goat? In my house?"

"Well, he said...he said the house belongs to him! He said he inherited it from his grandfather, Warlord the Goat."

The Hyena shrugged in utter disbelief. This must be a joke. "No goat would venture so far into the savanna, let alone claim my house! But we shall see!"

Together, Hyena and Monkey made their way to the house. As they approached, they heard strange sounds coming from within:

"MEAHHH! MEAHHH! MEAHHHHH!"

"Children, why are you making such noise?" Billy Goat asked loudly.

His wife answered in a louder voice. "The kids are hungry. I think they want some more hyena meat, my husband."

"Hyena meat?" Billy Goat responded. "But they had that fat, juicy hyena yesterday."

"Yes, but they say they want a fresh one. Growing children need their nourishment."

"Well then," declared Billy Goat, "tell them to be patient. That helpful monkey promised to bring a fat hyena right to our doorstep today. He mentioned this one is especially well-fed and tender!"

Outside in the darkness, Hyena froze. Her yellow eyes widened in horror as she slowly turned to look at Monkey.

"You... TRAITOR!" she snarled, her hackles rising. "Me, fat and tender? So you planned with them so they can have me for dinner?"

"What? No!" Monkey protested, bewildered. "I would never—" The Monkey sensed danger and jumped up into the trees and fled.

"I think I hear the Hyena, coming," said Billy Goat. Get ready, children."

"MEAHHH! MEAHHH! MEAHHHHH!"

Hyena heard the noise coming from his house and dashed off into the darkness.

Billy Goat and family had a peaceful night's rest and the next morning they found their way back to their own home.

For many seasons afterward, the tale of how Billy Goat outwitted the fearsome Hyena was told and retold around evening fires. And that is how wit triumphed over might in the heart of Hausaland.

4.

My Name Is Miriam Too!

Listen, my children, and hear this story of wit that saved two people from dangerous marauders in Rugu forest.

Not too far from here, in a small village near Rugu forest, lived Mati and his wife Miriam. They were good people who worked hard. Everyone who knew them loved them because they were kind and easygoing.

One day, during the harmattan season, Mati and Miriam decided to visit their relatives who lived in the big city beyond the forest. But to get to the city, they must travel through the dreaded Rugu forest.

Now, everyone in the village had heard stories about the terrible Rugu forest where the trees blocked out the sunlight, and day was like a moonless night. Many had gone through the forest and never returned. But what people feared the most about the forest was not the wild animals and the darkness—it was the notorious gang of armed robbers who used the forest as their hideout. Because of the atrocious activities of these armed robbers, the road had become almost impassable.

But Mati and Miriam had promised their relatives, and in our tradition, a promise is as sacred as the ancestral grounds. So, early in the morning, when the dew was not yet dry on the ground, they set out on their journey with courage in their hearts and prayers on their lips.

They walked quickly but quietly through the forest, but just as they got past the middle, their worst fears were confirmed as the armed bandits jumped down from the trees with bows and arrows and torches.

"Kneel! Now!" shouted the robbers in their gruff voices.

Mati and Mary dropped to their knees, their hearts beating fast like the *ganga* drums.

The gang leader raised his lighted torch and glowered at Mati and Miriam. He strolled toward Miriam, his footsteps heavy. He looked at her with eyes that had seen many terrible things.

"What's your name, and where are you going? Tell me now!"

Mati's wife was the first to find her voice. "My name is Miriam. We are going to see relatives in the city," she said, her voice trembling.

The gang leader paused and looked closer at her. "Did you say, Miriam?"

"Yes, Miriam. That's my name. Please don't hurt us. We just want to go visit our relatives."

The gang leader stood silent for a minute. "Well," he said finally, "Miriam is also my mother's name. She is so dear to me that I cannot harm anyone with the same name as hers. So I will spare you. Get up."

Miriam got up, still trembling with fright.

"But you," the gang leader growled and pointed a finger at Mati's face. "You, big for-nothing dude. Tell me your name!"

"My name is Miriam, too," the husband answered instinctively. "I swear, my name is Miriam, too."

The forest fell quiet. Then suddenly—HA HA HA!—the robbers burst into laughter! They laughed until tears rolled down their cheeks.

The gang leader looked at Mati and shook his head with amusement. "You are either the bravest or the most foolish man I have ever met," said the gang leader, wiping a tear from his eye. "But you have made us laugh today, and laughter is rare in this dark forest. For this—and for your wife's name—you may both continue your journey unharmed."

He ordered his men to return the couple's belongings and even provided them with fresh water for the rest of their journey.

5.

Halifa The Parrot Merchant

Once, there lived a middle-aged merchant in Hausaland named Halifa. He was known as a dealer in rare and exotic birds. Halifa favored parrots the most among all birds because of their fascinating personalities and ability to mimic how people talk.

"A parrot is really the best," Halifa would often say, "unlike other birds and even animals, the parrot can hold a conversation. A proper companion, if you ask me."

Halifa travelled to distant lands in search of the finest parrots to sell. During one of his journeys, he reached the country of the Barbers and lodged at the home of a wealthy merchant called Wazata.

One evening, as they shared a meal and talked about their trade, Wazata told Halifa that he should consider a journey to the land of the Arabs.

"Parrots are in high demand over there," Wazata said. "The sheiks pay handsome prices for talking parrots. Such birds are rare in their country and thus highly prized."

Although Halifa was excited by his host's advice, he was too tired from his travels to set out immediately. "I shall return home first to prepare properly for such a promising trade opportunity."

Halifa knew the journey to Arabia would take weeks and weeks and he also wanted some time to train his parrots. Furthermore, he would have to join a trade caravan traveling in that direction because of the risks and his lack of knowledge of the routes and terrains.

Upon returning to his homeland, Halifa selected his finest parrot and taught it some Arabic words. He trained the parrot to say greetings, tell jokes, and tell stories in Arabic. He thought the parrot talking in Arabic would fetch even a higher price in Arabia. When he was sure that the parrot had learned and memorized enough, he set out on his next task in preparation for the journey.

The next task for Halifa was to find a trade caravan that would travel to Arabia or somewhere in that direction. After days of searching and making inquiries, he finally found a caravan ready to begin the journey.

On the appointed date, the caravan set out with over a hundred merchants and carriers. Some rode on horses or camels while others walked, carrying their merchandise, food, and weapons for defense in case of attacks by marauders or wild animals. Halifa traveled on horseback, carrying his parrot in a beautiful cage.

After many weeks traveling through forests and mountains, the caravan finally reached the country of the Arabs. As was the custom in the land, foreign merchants had to camp outside the city until their goods were inspected and levies collected. The process took three days.

When they were finally allowed into the city, town criers went ahead of them and around the city to announce the arrival of the "merchants from distant lands with assorted and exotic merchandise!"

In no time, the courtyard at the guest inn where most foreign merchants lodged became a busy marketplace as the locals came to shop for attractive and rare commodities.

Halifa's stall, with its beautiful parrot in a glittering cage, quickly became the center of attraction.

"The finest of parrots, I tell you," Halifa proudly announced.

This parrot can greet you in the morning, tell jokes when you are bored, and all in your own language."

The onlookers were amazed and eager to hear the parrot speak.

"These are bold claims," a wealthy sheik said. "What price do you ask for such a remarkable bird?"

Halifa named a much higher price than he had initially thought, and the sheik agreed.

"I will pay your price," the sheik said, "but only after I have heard the parrot speak. Perhaps you can arrange a demonstration sometime?"

Halifa, confident in his parrot's abilities, suggested that the demonstration should take place the next day. "Bring anyone you wish to witness the parrot's performance," Halifa challenged.

That night, in his room at the inn, Halifa rehearsed with the parrot, and the parrot performed flawlessly. The bird sang the songs Halifa taught it and told jokes in Arabic. Halifa was sure the parrot would wow the onlookers the next day.

The next morning, the sheik, accompanied by spectators, gathered at Halifa's stall to watch the parrot perform.

When everybody was ready, Halifa brought out his parrot and showered him with praise, describing his breed, unique qualities, and worth.

"Now, my dear beautiful bird," Halifa said, "are all the things I said about you true? Speak to our wonderful guests, talk to them in their language so they can see for themselves how magnificent you are."

The crowd leaned forward in excitement, and everyone fell silent.

The parrot tilted his head left, then right, and then stretched his wings but remained silent.

Halifa cleared his throat, turned to the bird, and tried again to get the parrot to respond. Still, the parrot remained silent.

Some whispers and murmurs spread through the confused crowd.

Halifa smiled at the crowd. "Such a humble bird, this one. This parrot is not used to showing off, but give him some time."

Over and over again, Halifa tried to get the parrot to talk, but the parrot remained silent. Halifa was now visibly sweating. As the silence stretched uncomfortably, some onlookers began to laugh. The Sheik was looking disappointed and slightly angry by now. As the crowd watched, growing restless, the parrot began to shake and shiver as if he had fallen ill.

Halifa suspected that the parrot was only pretending, but he seized the opportunity to save himself more embarrassment.

"Ah, I see, oh poor bird," Halifa said in a pitying voice before turning to the crowd. "It seems the dear parrot is ill. I should have noticed. The poor bird must have caught the bird flu I heard has been affecting your lands."

The spectators were disappointed, but most believed the bird must have fallen ill. Halifa breathed a sigh of relief as the crowd began to disperse. The humiliation weighed on him like a heavy clock. With the shame, Halifa decided he would not wait for the caravan's scheduled departure. He waited in his room at the inn until midnight, and without telling anybody, he sneaked out and began the long journey back to his homeland.

As he headed for his country, many thoughts crossed his mind about what to do with the parrot. He considered letting the bird starve or throwing it away in the cage but decided not to.

After weeks of travel, Halifa finally got back home. Immediately, Halifa opened his door and walked into his house, the parrot began to sing:

My master took me,
To the country of the Arabs,
He wanted to sell me,
At a big price and for a reward,
And was desperate,
To make me speak,
But I refused!

6.

The Horned King And The Barber

Once, in a famous kingdom in Hausaland, ruled powerful King Tanko. Revered and feared by all in the kingdom, King Tanko had no rivals or enemies. Everyone paid obeisance and homage to him. But King Tanko had a secret: a mysterious horn that grew from the middle of his head. No one knew about this horn on the king's head, not even his family or closest advisers. The King was careful and made sure the horn stayed hidden under the crown he always wore.

King Tanko was so careful and determined to hide his secret that he broke a long-standing royal tradition by not appointing a royal barber. He preferred to shave his own head in secret, away from curious eyes.

Though his councilors and courtiers wondered why the king did not have a royal barber, as was the tradition, none dared approach the king on the matter.

After many years of shaving himself, King Tanko finally became tired of the task.

"What is the matter with me?" he said to himself. "I am the ruler of the greatest kingdom in all Hausaland. Must I lower myself to the work of a common barber when there are skilled men who would consider it an honor to shave my head? All because I have a horn. Have there not been many stories about great kings with tails, claws, and horns, which they bore with pride?"

The next morning, King Tanko summoned his vizier. "Find me the finest barber in all my domains," the king ordered. "The barber must also be one who can keep secrets."

After carefully searching throughout the kingdom, the vizier found Ali the barber, known for his skill as a barber and for his reserved and quiet nature.

Shortly after that, when the king became due for another head shave, he sent for the new royal barber, Ali. When Ali came to the palace, the royal guards led him to a secluded garden where King Tanko sat waiting. When the king saw the barber approach, he dismissed all his attendants with a wave. When they were alone, King Tanko sat on a stool and took off his crown so Ali could do his duty.

Ali the barber gasped in shock when he saw the horn protruding from the king's head. He began to tremble. He would have run off, but his legs refused to move.

"Calm down," the king said to Ali, "no need to be so shocked." The king sighed as he continued. "Kings are blessed with miracles in varying forms, you know. Some kings have horns, others have tails, and some have claws. Yet, we are still humans. So do not panic."

Despite the king's reassurances, Ali was so frightened by the horn that he continued to tremble so violently that he could barely hold his barbing tools.

With a sigh of resignation, King Tanko told Ali the barber to leave. But the king warned the barber to never speak of what he had seen.

Ali left the palace, and for many weeks, he kept the king's secret to himself, despite being haunted by it day and night. However, as time went by, the secret weighed heavily on Ali's mind until he could no longer resist the urge to speak it out. Ali soon came up with an idea to relieve himself of the king's secret without anyone pointing an accusing finger at him.

With his new idea, the next morning, Ali went to his small plot of farmland near the outskirts of his village. There, with no one near, he began to plant corn seeds. As he placed each seed in the soil, he whispered a song into the earth:

"Miracle, miracle, miracle
The kings, emperors, and saints
Have them in varying forms
Horns, tails, or claws
My king, my dear king, is also blessed
A mysterious horn

In the middle of his head
Beneath the crown."

After whispering the king's secret into the ground, Ali felt very relieved.

Time went by, and the corn crops grew. After they were harvested, children used the dried corn stalks to make flutes as they did every year during harvest season.

But when the children blew the flutes, instead of the usual sounds, the flutes played the words Ali had whispered when he planted the seeds.

"Miracle, miracle, miracle
The kings, emperors, and saints
Have them in varying forms
Horns, tails, or claws
My king, my dear king, is also blessed
A mysterious horn
In the middle of his head
Beneath the crown."

Soon, the songs about King Tanko having a horn spread rapidly and widely throughout the kingdom until news of it reached the king's ears.

7.

The Judge's Decree

In a small village not too far away, two men, Nda and Bawa were arrested for public disturbance and brought before the local judge. While Nda was a simple farmer who had never learned to read or write, Bawa had received some formal education.

When the charge was read to them, they both pleaded guilty to the offence. The judge, therefore, decided to hold a summary trial and pass a sentence.

On this particular day, however, the judge was in an unusually good mood.

"Today is a happy day for me," the judge said. "My home has been blessed with a child after many years of trying. So, because I am in a generous mood, I will not send you to prison.

Instead, each one of you will be given twenty lashes. And you are free to choose how you want the whipping. I promise to abide by whatever you choose."

Nda was the first to speak. "Your Honor, I request to receive my lashes while wearing my full clothes."

The judge nodded. "Granted."

Nda was made to lie face down on a table in the front of the courtroom, and he received his lashes.

When it was Bawa's turn, Bawa made an odd request. "Your honor," he said, "I request to receive my lashes while Nda lies on top of me."

On hearing Bawa's request, Nda began to protest. "Your honor, that is unfair," Nda said. "Please do not allow this!"

"Well," the judge said, "I did promise to abide by how you chose to receive your whipping. I am sorry, Nda, but you must lie on top of Bawa while he receives his lashes."

And so, Nda was made to lie on top of Bawa on the table to receive twenty more lashes.

8.

The Jackal's Foresight

A long time ago, as people became more skilled in hunting, Lion, the King of the Jungle, invited Snake, Tiger, and Jackal to an important meeting at his lair.

When they were assembled, the Lion told them he wanted them to stay together at his lair so that they would be less vulnerable to ambush by hunters.

The Snake and the Tiger welcomed the idea and agreed to do as suggested by the Lion. The Jackal, however, politely declined. Though the Jackal gave some excuse for his decision, he privately doubted that such powerful animals could all live together peacefully.

Before the Lion, the Snake, and the Tiger moved in together, they agreed to lay down some conditions.

The Lion was the first to state his conditions. "You all know that I am the King of the Jungle," he said. "I will take no nonsense from anyone. Anyone who wants to stay with me must respect me," he roared.

The Tiger was next. "I dislike being stared at," she said. "Look at me only once, and briefly, or face my hot temper."

"Whatever you do," said the Snake, "do not touch my tail. "If you do that, I am certain to lose my patience."

All three accepted the conditions with a vow to abide by them.

Not too long after, the Lion had an unlucky day and could not prey on anything. When he made it back to the lair, he was hungry, exhausted, and irritable.

Soon after, the Tiger returned from her hunt and went to lie in her corner. The Snake soon also crawled in.

"Greetings, friends," hissed the Snake when he slithered into the lair. His greeting, however, went unanswered.

By this time, the Tiger had noticed that the Lion's eyes had not left her since she entered.

"I do not like being stared at," she told the Lion. "Perhaps you have forgotten my condition."

The Lion ignored her and continued to stare at her.

"I do not like being stared at," she repeated, her voice rising. "Stop staring at me!"

The Lion felt disrespected by the Tiger's raised voice, so he roared and launched himself at her. A ferocious battle ensued between the two cats. They slashed and clawed at each other, and in the chaos, they rolled over to where Snake was quietly watching. Before Snake could get out of the way, the Lion's heavy paw fell heavily on the Snake's tail. The pain caused the Snake to instinctively strike the lion and sink his fangs into the Lion's leg.

The venom immediately took effect on the Lion and he staggered back and collapsed in a corner. The Tiger too, severely wounded from the fight with the Lion also staggered and fell to the side. The Snake, in much pain from his crushed tail slithered to a corner and lay still.

And so it was that when dawn broke the following day, the Jackal, passing by on his morning hunt, found the three creatures lying still in the lair.

"Alas," the Jackal sighed, shaking his head sadly. "I saw this coming."

9.

Moyi's Ten Lessons

Once, there lived a boy named Moyi. When his father lay sick and dying, he summoned Moyi and sent him on an important errand to a friend.

"Go and return quickly before I die," his father said, "for I must tell you ten lessons that will guide you through life."

Moyi ran as fast as he could, but when he returned, he found that his father had already passed away. Heartbroken, Moyi wept and wept and wept.

After his tears had eased, Moyi resolved to travel the world and not return home until he discovered the ten life lessons his father had meant to share with him.

At daybreak, Moyi set out into the forest.

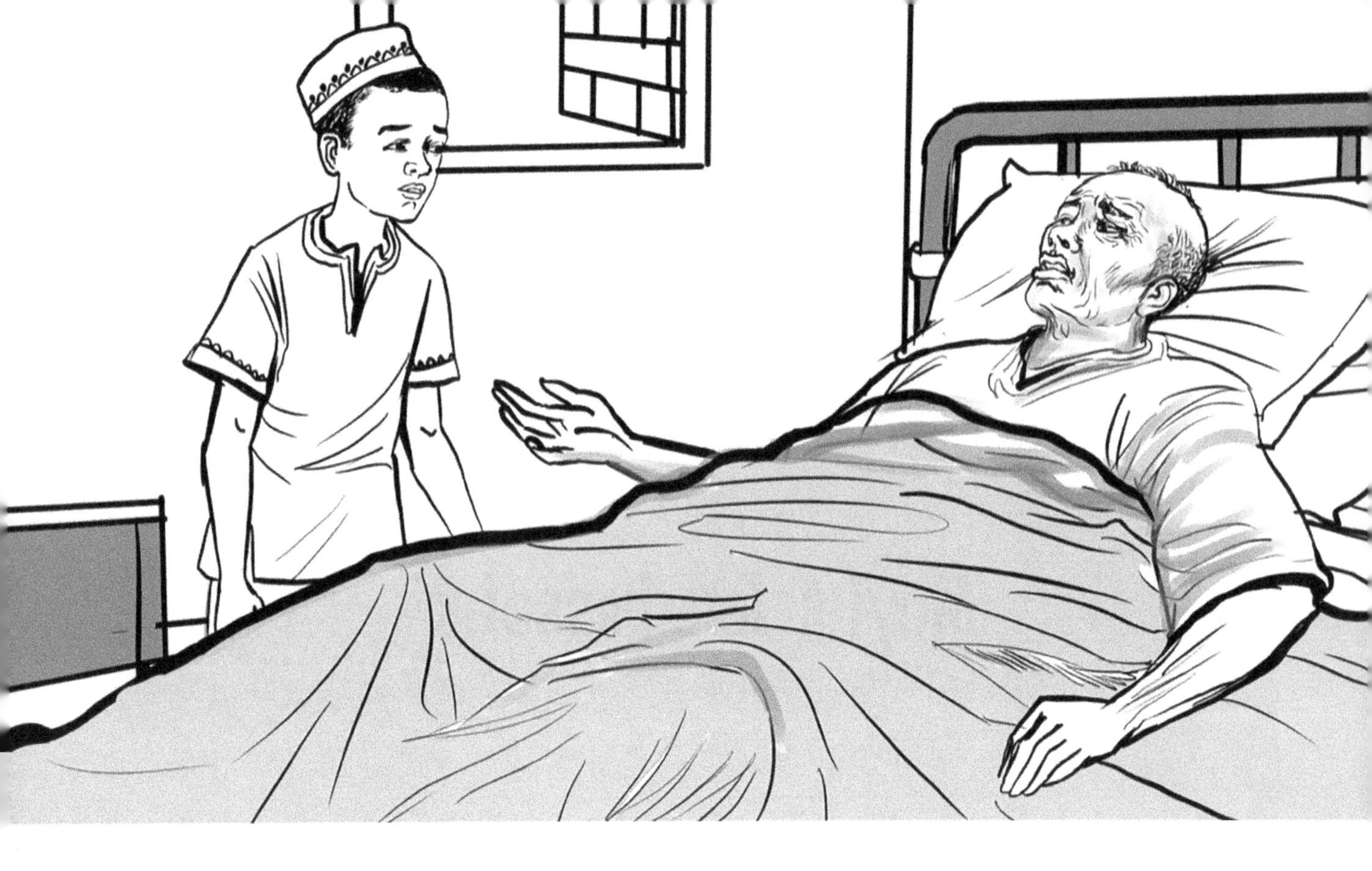

As he traveled, tears still flowed down his cheeks at the loss of his father. Soon, he met a Hyena who noticed his tears.

"What is the matter, child?" inquired the Hyena when she saw Moyi's tears.

Moyi told the Hyena his story. The Hyena nodded sympathetically.

"I can share one of those ten lessons with you," said the Hyena. "The lesson I will teach you is that *you should never be greedy or covet what belongs to others;* otherwise, everyone will despise you. Look at me—I am despised by people, not for any wrong I have done to them, but because they perceive me as greedy.

Moyi thanked the Hyena and continued his journey.

After a long walk, he came across an old Horse. When the Horse saw him crying, he stopped and asked what the matter was. After hearing Moyi's tale, the Horse said, "I, too, have a lesson for you. It is a lesson from my life. If you hold onto it, you will be fulfilled and end well. Here is the lesson: *Whatever you wish to accomplish in life, do it in the prime of your youth. In old age, strength fails, and you may find yourself irrelevant and abandoned, even by those closest to you.*"

After thanking the Horse for the lesson, Moyi walked on until he got to a mountain where he met a Snake. Before the Snake could say anything, Moyi shared his story.

"I will share one important lesson with you," said the Snake. "*Never hurt anyone unless you have no choice.* Consider my situation," continued the Snake, "despite being one of the most beautiful creatures, most people still despise me. I am regarded as an enemy. I am always hiding or running from those who would hurt me at first sight."

"Thank you," Moyi said to the Snake and went on his way.

He soon got to a stream where he found the Dog trying to cross over. On seeing him, the Dog asked what he was doing alone in the forest. After Moyi explained his mission, the Dog said he had one lesson to teach him.

"Be loyal to your master and never betray anyone, no matter the cost," the Dog warned. "Loyalty pays, but betrayal does not."

Moyi thanked the Dog and resumed his journey.

As Moyi traversed through the forest, there came the ant, who, after listening to Moyi, shared a lesson with him. "*When you have a task too great for you alone, get others to help. What one cannot accomplish, many can achieve together.*" The ant continued, "You see how we ants, as tiny as we are, can move things many times our size when we unite and join hands? Together we can even push an elephant."

Proceeding further, Moyi spotted a Hoopoe perched on a tree branch. He raised his head in greetings and told the Hoopoe about his mission.

The Hoopoe advised him thus: *"Seek knowledge wherever you can find it, for it is the key to greatness. Remember that wealth may decrease, and authority or power may be lost, but knowledge is permanent."*

"Thank you," Moyi said and moved along.

As he walked on, a Tortoise called out to him.

After hearing Moyi's story, the Tortoise shared her wisdom: *"Do not be hasty in life. Remember that slow and steady wins the race."*

After leaving the Tortoise, Moyi turned eastward. Traveling on this new path, he soon met the Camel.

After hearing his story, the Camel gave Moyi another lesson. *"My lesson for you is that you should live simply and practice obedience,"* the camel said. "Learn this from me," continued the Camel. "My simplicity and obedience save me from harsh treatment, so that even a small boy can drive me anywhere without difficulty."

Shortly after, as Moyi continued his journey, he met the Monitor Lizard, who wondered what the boy was doing in the forest. Hearing Moyi's story, the Monitor Lizard advised: *"Be patient and tolerant in all situations. Always remember that no condition is permanent."*

With nine lessons collected, Moyi decided to head home, hoping to discover the tenth lesson on his return journey. As he neared the end of the forest, he met the Jackal, who wanted to know what the boy was doing in the forest. Moyi explained his journey and mentioned that he had collected nine lessons so far.

The Jackal smiled. "Then I shall give you the tenth. The tenth lesson is this: *consider all these lessons as your father's own words and always put them into practice."*

"Thank you," Moyi said to the Jackal.

With gratitude in his heart and wisdom in his mind, Moyi returned home with the ten lessons that would guide him throughout his life.

10.

Mallam Dogo And The Spider

Once upon a time, there lived a man named Mallam Dogo who was said to be the tallest person in Hausaland. No one could see or even reach the top of his head, which was as high as some treetops. But Mallam Dogo was wicked and dubious and took advantage of his height to intimidate and defraud people.

One day, Mallam Dogo decided that he needed a servant, but he was too miserly to spend money to hire someone. After thinking about it, he came up with an idea by which he could get one for free.

The next market day, when traders from far and wide came to the town square to trade, Mallam Dogo took his heftiest bull to the market. Standing at the center of the market from where he could see everyone, he began to call out loudly:

"A bull for free! A bull for free! Whoever wants this fine bull, come forward now!"

People quickly gathered around him, as everyone wanted the bull. When Mallam Dogo saw that many people had gathered with interest in the bull, he cleared his throat and called for silence.

"The bull is indeed free," he declared, "but with one condition."

"Let us hear the condition," the people said.

"Now, listen carefully," Mallam Dogo told the crowd. "It is all quite simple. I will give this bull right now to anyone who wants it. But after a week, I will visit the new owner, and if the new owner can touch the top of my head, the bull becomes theirs permanently. But if this new owner fails to touch my head, then he will become my servant for life."

When they heard the condition, the people began to disperse, as they knew that it was impossible for anyone to touch the top of Mallam Dogo's head.

As the crowd thinned, a small spider called out to Mallam Dogo and told him he would accept the challenge.

"I accept your offer," the Spider declared. "I will take ownership of the bull right away."

"Very well," replied Mallam Dogo with a cunning smile.

People in the crowd tried to talk the Spider out of it, especially as some knew of Mallam Dogo's shady reputation. But the Spider only smiled. Not many knew that the Spider was very cunning and that he already planned to outsmart Mallam Dogo.

Spider took the bull home and hosted a feast. Many came to enjoy the food, though they worried about Spider's fate.

A week later, as agreed, Mallam Dogo made his way to Spider's house. He was followed by curious people eager to see what would happen.

"I have arrived," Mallam Dogo shouted when he got to Spider's house. "Come out now, you coward. No need to hide."

"I am not hiding," the Spider replied from inside the house. "I am just trying to finish a small but important task. I will be out soon enough."

"What important task is that?" Mallam Dogo asked impatiently.

"Well, I am trying to stitch a crack on the wall of my room with a needle and thread," said the Spider.

"You liar," Mallam Dogo said, growing even angrier. "How can anyone stitch a wall with a needle and thread?"

"It is very much possible," replied the Spider calmly. "In this very town, some have the skill. If you don't believe me, you can come have a look if you like."

Angry and irritated by what he thought was the Spider's attempt to delay becoming his servant, Mallam Dogo poked his head through the low window to see what the Spider was up to. This was precisely what the Spider was waiting for. Before Mallam Dogo knew what was happening, the Spider jumped up and touched the top of Mallam Dogo's head.

"I did it," the Spider shouted in triumph. "People, look, I did it. I have touched Mallam Dogo's head. The bull is now mine permanently!"

The People cheered at the Spider's wit and Mallam Dogo stomped off in shame.

From that day forward, the story spread far and wide about how the tiny Spider defeated the tallest man in Hausaland—not through strength, but by wit.

11.

Why Animals Act Like They Do

A long time ago, the Donkey, the Goat, and the dog were very good friends. They spent most of their time together, playing or just chatting. One day, they grew bored and began to wonder what lay beyond the familiar surroundings of their village.

"Well, we could find out," said the Goat. "We could take a trip, if you are both up for it."

The others got excited and agreed. But as they planned the trip, they realized that the trip would be too long to travel on foot. "We should use the public transport," the Donkey suggested, "It will save us time and we will get to see more."

The friends all agreed to this.

When the day of departure arrived, the three friends went to the motor park and boarded a vehicle bound for their first destination. The journey was pleasant, with interesting scenery passing by their windows. They chatted excitedly about what they saw through the windows and the adventures they would have in the places they would visit.

When they got to their first stop, the conductor asked for their fare as they got off the vehicle. “One pound each,” the conductor told them.

The Donkey was the first to pay. He pulled out his wallet, gave a one-pound note to the conductor, and got off.

The Goat got off and reached for her purse. After patting her pockets and checking her bag, she realized she had left home without it. Before anyone could stop her, she took off running and disappeared among the crowd at the station.

The Dog got off next, and when he pulled out his wallet, he saw that he had no small denominations. "I only have a five-pound note," he explained, handing the money to the conductor. "I'll need four pounds in change, please."

But as the Dog was waiting for the conductor to hand him the change, the driver drove off.

"Hey! Wait! My change!" the dog barked, trying to chase the vehicle as it sped off.

Later that day, the three friends reunited and decided to continue their journey on foot. As they walked around, they soon noticed that they were each acting strangely.

The Donkey would walk or sit in the middle of the road and not give way to any vehicle. He believed that since he had paid his transport fare, he could use the road however he pleased.

As for the Dog, each time a vehicle came by, he would start barking and chasing after the vehicle, asking for his change.

The Goat was also behaving differently. Each time a vehicle approached, the Goat would take off running because she still did not have the transport fare.

And so it is to this very day.

12.

How The Rodent Was Betrayed By Her Tail

One day, a hungry Rodent sneaked into Ahmad's house to steal some food. While creeping quietly and sniffing pots and pans, the Rodent accidentally knocked down a dish, which made a loud noise as it fell and rolled down the kitchen floor.

The noise startled Ahmad, who jumped up and ran into the kitchen. There, he found the Rodent frozen and looking wide-eyed in fear. Ahmad dashed after the Rodent, hoping to trap it, but the Rodent ran off and escaped into a hole in the wall.

Inside the hole in the wall, the Rodent sighed in relief. "That was close," she thought. "I almost got caught."

But unknown to the Rodent, her tail was still dangling from the hole in the wall.

Ahmad thought the Rodent had escaped and had almost given up his search when he saw the hole in the wall and the rodent's tail dangling like a corn stalk in the wind.

"There you are," he said as he reached down quickly, grabbed the protruding tail, and pulled the rodent out of the hole.

Ahmad severely punished the Rodent before letting it go. "That will teach you," he said as he let her run off.

From that day, the Rodent nursed a bitter grudge against her tail. And whenever she met her friends, she would warn them not to trust their tails. "Beware of your tails," she would say, "for your enemy is always at your back. Your tails are at your back!"

13.

The Clever Princess Of Musawa

Many, many years ago, in the kingdom of Musawa in Hausaland, reigned a king whose daughter Rabi'atu—known affectionately as Princess Rabi of Alkalawa—possessed not only extraordinary beauty but also a formidable intellect that distinguished her among her peers.

When Princess Rabi reached marriageable age, countless suitors from far and near came to ask for her hand in marriage, but she turned them all down. Her father, the king, was troubled by her refusal to get married, but because he loved her dearly and did not want to hurt her feelings, he was reluctant to bring up the subject or put pressure on her.

However, as time passed and Princess Rabi did not pick a suitor, the king began to worry about the kingdom's future. The princess was his sole heir and would one day inherit the throne.

"An unmarried woman to inherit the throne was unheard of," the king muttered as he sat alone in the royal garden.

The next day, the king summoned the princess and reluctantly told her about his worries concerning her refusal to pick a suitor.

On noticing the worries in her father's face, Princess Rabi knelt before him and placed her hands on his knees.

"Your Majesty," she said respectfully, "I appreciate your concerns for my future and that of our beloved kingdom. I promise I will never bring shame to you or the kingdom, but I am resolved to marry only the right person at the right time."

"My princess," said the king, "don't be childish. All the suitable men in this kingdom have proposed to you, and you've rejected them all. Among them were princes, merchants, men of wisdom, and warriors. Who else do you want?"

"Yes, Your Majesty, you are right," Princess Rabi replied, "but forgive me, I am looking for a husband who will not treat me as chattel and discard me when he tires of me."

"How would you know such a person by mere appearance?" the king asked.

"I have an idea already," Princess Rabi replied. "If Your Majesty pleases, I will conduct a small contest for my suitors. If I succeed, I'll have what I want. If not, I'll try another method until I find the right man."

"Now, my dear princess," the king said, "tell me what you are up to and how I can be of help."

"First," she explained, "I want your majesty to send word out that I will hold a contest. All my suitors must be there, and whoever among them wins the contest will have my hand in marriage."

The king chuckled. "Contest! What contest? Archery, horse racing, fencing, or what?"

"None of those," the princess replied, "just a simple dressing contest. I want a man who can dress properly and better than all others."

"Nonsense!" the king exclaimed. "A fashion show for such an important decision? Well, not in my lifetime!"

Princess Rabi remained calm. "Not at all, Your Majesty," she said. "My plan is to provide each contestant with new clothes and ask him to put them on. It's not the clothes that matter, but how they are worn."

"Can anyone not put on new clothes?" asked the king.

"Here is my point," she explained. "The man who throws away his old clothes because he has new ones is not the same as the one who puts new clothes over the old. The former's attitude shows he would discard me as his wife if he finds another woman, whereas the latter shows he values what he already possesses."

The king finally agreed and ordered the town crier to announce the contest throughout the kingdom.

On the day of the contest, each suitor was provided with a set of fine new clothes. Some removed their original garments before donning the new ones, and some even tore and discarded their old clothes to put on the new.

But one thoughtful suitor simply put the new clothes over what he was already wearing. When all had finished, Princess Rabi declared him the winner, and they were married in an elaborate and lavish ceremony.

14.

The Threacherous Three

Once upon a time, a Snake slithered into a village to avenge the killing of his wife. When the villagers saw him, they grabbed their sticks and went after the Snake. The Snake ran as fast as he could, but the villagers kept up the pursuit.

The Snake was out of breath and was about to give up when he spotted a Hippie by the roadside.

"Oh, Hippie," gasped the snake, "protect me. Save my life!"

The Hippie told the Snake to take cover behind him. But the Snake thought that he would not be safe there.

"They'll find me there," hissed the Snake. "Open your mouth and let me inside—they'll never look for me there!"

At first, the Hippie hesitated, but when he saw the villagers fast approaching with sticks, he immediately opened his mouth and let the Snake in.

When the villagers arrived and saw the Hippie, they asked him if he had seen the Snake.

"I believe I saw one slithering into the forest about an hour ago."

On hearing that, the villagers decided to give up the chase and return to the village. Once they were gone, the Hippie asked the Snake to come out and be on his way.

"You are safe now," the Hippie said. "They are gone."

But the Snake, now quite comfortable in his warm hideaway,

replied. “Come out? Why would I leave? I couldn’t find a better place than this! I think I’ll stay and feast on your liver and kidneys.”

The Hippie tried every trick to get the Snake out. He pleaded, reasoned, and even threatened, but the Snake refused to come out. The Hippie knew he was in big trouble, so he began to scream for help.

The Hawk happened to be flying by when he heard the Hippie screaming for help. “What is the matter?” asked the Hawk, landing beside the Hippie.

The Hippie explained his predicament. He narrated how he had saved the Snake’s life only to be repaid with treachery.

The Hawk nodded with sympathy and understanding and offered to help the Hippie.

“At midday tomorrow,” the Hawk said, “you should lie on your back and open your mouth as wide as you can toward the sun. Your stomach will become so hot that the Snake won’t be able to bear it, so he will be forced to come out. I will hide nearby and seize the Snake as soon as he appears.”

The next day at midday, the Hippie did as he was told by the Hawk. Within a few minutes, when the midday sun heated his stomach, the Snake could no longer stand the heat and began to wriggle toward the Hippie’s mouth. As soon as the Snake’s head emerged, the Hawk seized him by the head and pulled him out.

After the Snake had been dealt with, the Hawk recommended that the Hippie eat two chickens as remedy for the wounds done to his organs by the Snake.

As the Hawk was set to leave, the Hippie swiftly knocked him down and trapped him in a net. "Now," the Hippie said, "I have one chicken at hand and I will go look for the second one to do as you have advised." The Hippie dragged the Hawk back home and locked him in a chicken coop before leaving to hunt for another chicken.

While he was gone, the Hippie's wife discovered the Hawk locked up by her husband.

"Why are you locked up here?" she asked, concerned.

The Hawk explained his predicament. He narrated how he had saved the Hippie's life only to be repaid with treachery.

The Hippie's wife nodded with sympathy and understanding and offered to help the Hawk.

But as soon as she unlocked the coop, the Hawk pounced on her.

15.

How The Jackal Became A Teacher

A long time ago, the inhabitants of Runka village were hit by a severe famine caused by years of drought. To avoid starvation, the villagers began to hunt the animals from the nearby forest. As the hunting intensified, the animals worried that they were gradually sliding into extinction.

To discuss how the animals could protect themselves against the hunters, the Lion, king of the forest, called an urgent meeting at his palace.

When they were all assembled, the Lion asked each animal to share strategies for how they would avoid the hunters.

The Hare was the first to share his strategy. "When the villagers' dogs come after me," the Hare said, "I run as fast as I can and dart from side to side until I find a mound to hide behind."

"Mtcheew," the elephant sighed, interrupting the Hare. "Dogs don't worry me," the Elephant said dismissively, "but what mound could possibly conceal someone of my stature?"

More animals shared their escape and defensive strategies until it came to the Jackal's turn.

"There are three situations when we're most vulnerable to attack," the jackal said: "when we are drinking at the watering hole or lake, when we are sleeping, and when we are searching for food."

The Tiger looked at the Jackal. "Okay, what's your point?" said the Tiger. "Are you suggesting we should not drink water, eat, or sleep? That's impossible."

"My suggestion," said the Jackal patiently, "is that we take more specific precautions at those times."

"What sort of precautions would you suggest?" asked the Lion.

"Your majesty," the Jackal said. "First, I do not drink water openly like you all do. When I go to the lake to drink, I turn my head to face the road, dip my tail in the water, and lick the water from it until my thirst is quenched. Second, I sleep only on flat, dry ground where I can hear even the slightest sound—even a falling needle would wake me. Third, I avoid eating at unusual places, no matter how hungry I am. I only go for my food if I find it in the usual places."

The animals nodded and expressed their admiration for Jackal's strategies.

"These are very good Ideas," the Lion said. "I propose that we establish a school and appoint the Jackal to teach these survival skills to all animals."

And this was how the Jackal became a teacher!

16.

The Clever Wizard

Once upon a time, when a very beloved king died, the entire kingdom was thrown into mourning. For many weeks, there was no sound of laughing children playing or the noise of traders in the market square, even the animals were quiet as the kingdom grieved. In due time, according to custom, the eldest son of the late king was appointed to succeed his father on the throne, but the kingdom still remained somber.

The new king was so heartbroken by the death of his father, the late king, that he offered a great reward to anyone who could bring the late king back from the dead.

Around this period, a famous wizard stopped by the kingdom for a visit and found everyone still grieving and somber.

When he heard of the death of the old king and of the young king's generous reward, he went to the palace and requested an audience with the young king.

"Your Majesty," the wizard said with a bow, "I heard about your reward, and I have come to humbly offer my services. You see, I am a wizard of extraordinary powers, and resurrecting the dead is only a small matter."

The king nodded. "I did promise to reward anyone who can return my father to life," the king said, "but I also promised that those who take up my offer and fail will face severe consequences."

The wizard bowed. "Understood, Your Majesty. If you would like a demonstration of my abilities, may I humbly ask that you close your eyes?"

The king closed his eyes and when he opened them moments later, he found himself in an entirely different but magnificent city. The city was unlike any he had ever seen. The wizard took the king on a tour of this magnificent city and after the tour, he asked the king to shut his eyes again, and in an instant, they were back to the palace.

Sufficiently impressed, the king permitted the wizard to attempt to bring back his late father, the late king, from the dead. They proceeded to the late king's grave, accompanied by trusted witnesses.

At the royal cemetery, the wizard knelt before the late king's grave and began muttering incantations. From time to time, he would tilt his head or nod as if engaged in conversation with the deceased.

"Your Majesty," the wizard called into the grave. "I bring salutations from your son, the new king." The wizard paused as if listening to a reply from the grave. "Yes, your son. He is here with me," the wizard continued. "He is heartbroken and wishes for you to come back to life. Are you ready to come back to life or should I give you some time?" The wizard paused as if listening. "Oh, I see," said the wizard moments later. "Yes, Your Majesty, I will pass the message."

"Well," the young king asked, looking at the wizard impatiently, "what did my father say? What message did he give you for me?"

"Your Majesty," replied the wizard, "when I conveyed your wish to your father, he said to tell you that he is in great comfort in the afterlife. However, he has agreed to return on one condition: you must relinquish the throne to him and return to your position as prince. That is his only condition, and it is not negotiable."

The young king remained silent for a moment as he pondered the conditions. "My father is being selfish," he finally said. "How can one live a full life and still want to live the life of others. I think that is unrealistic and greedy of him. Tell him that since he is comfortable where he is, let him stay there."

Though disappointed, the king still rewarded the wizard generously for his effort. He never realized the wizard's clever deception.

17.

The Ungrateful Three

One day, an Angel descended from the heavens disguised as a human. The Angel's mission was to test how humans would react to different conditions or new opportunities.

The Angel first visited a Leper. "Make any wish," the Angel said to the Leper, "and it shall be granted."

The Leper wasted no time. "Free me from this leprosy," he said, "and grant me wealth."

The Angel offered some prayers and the Leper was cured. The Angel also blessed him with abundant riches.

The Angel disappeared and went next to the house of a man with a curved spine. There, too, the Angel asked the man to make any wish, and it would be granted.

“I wish only to stand straight like other people,” was the man’s wish.

The Angel prayed and the man was instantly cured.

From there, the Angel proceeded to a blind’ man’s home. When the Angel told him his mission and asked him to make a wish, the Blind man requested to have his vision restored.

The Angel prayed and the Blind man regained his eyesight.

All three people the Angel visited were not only cured of their ailments but also blessed with riches.

After one year, the Angel returned to earth again and paid a visit to all three people who had been cured a year earlier. The Angel first disguised himself as a leper and went to the former Leper's mansion.

When the former Leper saw the Angel in the shape of a leper, he immediately ordered his servant to send him away.

"Tell him never to return here!" he commanded. "I cannot bear the sight of lepers in my home."

The Angel went away disappointed.

The Angel next transformed into a man with a curved spine and visited the home of the man who used to have a curved spine. Like the first, this man scornfully rejected the visitor, unwilling to be reminded of his former state.

Finally, the Angel took the appearance of a blind man and visited the Blind man whom he had cured. The formerly Blind man received the blind visitor with open arms. He treated him very well and told him that he too used to be in the same condition and therefore regarded every blind man as his brethren.

The Angel thanked him and left.

The next morning, the former Leper and the man healed of a curved spine returned to their previous conditions as punishment for their ungratefulness.

18.

The Scorpion And The Snake

Once upon a time, the Scorpion felt that her poison was not as potent as she wanted it to be. She believed she needed a stronger, more powerful poison to better protect her from enemies, so she went to the Snake, who was known for his very potent venom.

When the Scorpion arrived at the Snake's home, she saw that he wasn't home. Rather than return later, she slipped inside to wait and settled herself near the entrance.

A few minutes later, the Snake returned. While entering his house, he accidentally slithered over the Scorpion waiting just inside the entrance. The Scorpion instinctively struck and stung the Snake, who began to twist and shudder from the pain.

"My apologies," the Scorpion said, "I reacted instinctively. I am sorry."

When the pain subsided, the Snake asked the Scorpion what she was doing in his house.

"I came to ask a favor," explained the Scorpion. "I wanted you to give me some of your venom to make mine more potent so I could better defend myself."

The Snake thought about it for a moment and then shook his head.

"No," said the Snake, "I am sorry, but I can't give you any venom because you are far too hot-tempered. You could easily hurt an innocent person. Learn to control your temper."

The Snake bid the disappointed Scorpion farewell and sent her away.

19.

The Farmer And The Devil

A Farmer who had gone to his farm to work found some men gambling under the shade tree on his farmland. The leader of the gamblers was the Devil himself, but no one recognized him because he had disguised himself as a gentleman.

The Farmer asked the men to stop gambling and leave, but they ignored him. After the Farmer's repeated pleas failed, he decided to force them to leave by cutting down the tree. He took out his axe and began chopping on the tree's stem.

The Devil told the Farmer to stop, but the Farmer ignored him. When the Farmer refused to stop, the Devil snatched the axe from him and pushed him down. The Farmer got up and hit the Devil, and they began to fight.

Though the Devil seemed stronger, the Farmer succeeded in overpowering him and knocking him down. As the Farmer raised his axe to hit the Devil, the Devil pleaded for mercy. The Devil told the Farmer that if he spared him, he would reward him with a secret for making money without the hard work of farming.

When the Farmer agreed and released him, the Devil told the Farmer that if he checked under his pillow every morning, he would find five shillings.

The next morning, the Farmer checked under his pillow and found the money. And every morning after that, the Farmer would check under his pillow and pick up the money. He soon became very rich.

One morning, the Farmer looked under his pillow as usual but found nothing. He checked again the next day but again found nothing. He then decided to go to his farm. When he got to the farm, he saw the Devil and his friends gambling again under the shade tree. Without saying a word, he pulled out his axe and started chopping the tree.

The Devil shouted at the Farmer to stop, but the Farmer ignored him. The Devil snatched the axe from the Farmer, knocked him down, and threatened to kill him. The Farmer begged the Devil to spare him.

When the Devil relented and spared the Farmer's life, the Farmer was quite surprised.

"When we fought the last time," the Famer said, "I overpowered you though you were much stronger. Now I am much stronger, yet you have subdued me. Why?"

"When we fought the last time," the Devil replied, "you fought in good faith, which is why you won. But now you are fighting because you lost the money you have been collecting. You are not fighting for a just cause but for the sake of money."

20.

The Big Liars

There once lived a man renowned for his ability to tell the biggest and most convincing lies. No one was known to have ever matched or bested him in a lie.

One day, this renowned liar took a trip to a neighboring town. Along the way, he met a woman tending the garden in front of her house.

"Excuse me," said the big liar, "have you seen a pregnant antelope around these parts?"

"What about the pregnant antelope?" the woman asked with curiosity.

The big liar replied, "Well, I shot her with my arrow, and though the arrow narrowly missed the antelope, it still struck the fetus she was carrying inside her stomach. I heard the fetus bleat."

The woman smiled knowingly and replied, "Well, I had no time to notice the antelope because I have been busy separating the cold water from the hot water, which the maids accidentally mixed.

Author the Author

Born and educated in Northern Nigeria, Abubakar Yusuf Ibrahim is a distinguished author with a passion for storytelling. He studied law at the University of Sokoto and embarked on his writing journey in 1983 with the playbook *Kaico*. Known for his engaging narratives and cultural insights, Abubakar has contributed significantly to African literature with works such as *Kundin Wakoki*, a collection of poems that explore diverse themes. Abubakar's stories reflect his dedication to preserving and sharing the rich perspectives of Hausa culture with audiences young and old. He lives in Katsina, Nigeria.